MW00872824

Reindeer Dust™

By
Kate Dwyer

illustrated by
Joanne Lew-Vriethoff

Reindeer Dust

Reindeer Dust
Copyright © 2014 Reindeer Dust, Inc.

All rights reserved. Published by Reindeer Dust Press. Reindeer Dust and associated logos are trademarks of Reindeer Dust, Inc.

Printed in the USA
ISBN 978-0-9893176-0-3

Illustrated by Joanne Lew-Vriethoff
Designed by Jess Lam

Library of Congress Control Number: 2014901587

No part of this book may be used or reproduced by any means without written permission of the publisher. For information regarding written permission, write to Reindeer Dust Press, 1500 Lanier Place NE, Atlanta, Georgia 30306. www.reindeerdust.com

Printed in the United States by Bookmasters
30 Amberwood Parkway
Ashland, OH 44805
July 2014
50005160

To my family, who fills my life with magic, and to Lori,
Abigail and Ann for adding their sparkling touch.

A special thank-you to our neighbors Linda and Johnny
for inviting us to share in their Reindeer Dust tradition.

- K. D.

For Max and Mattiece who continue to inspire me everyday with their
very own made up crazy stories and art. Thank you for your cookies,
cakes and soups that kept me going through the many late nights.
I love you, my babies.

- J. L. V.

The magic began one storied Christmas Eve.
Santa had presents; he was ready to leave.

His sled was packed full, spilling over the rim
with treasures and gifts adorned in stylish trim.

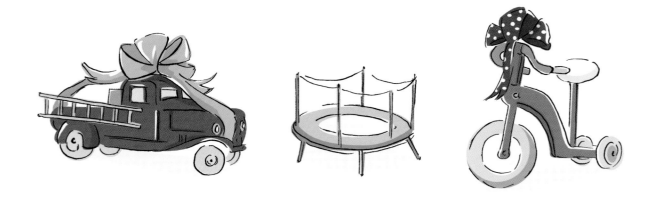

There were trucks and trampolines, bikes, bats and balls,

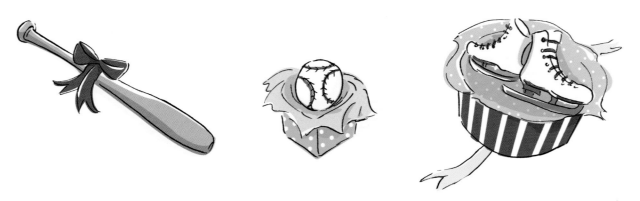

scooters, skates and skis, darling dresses and dolls.

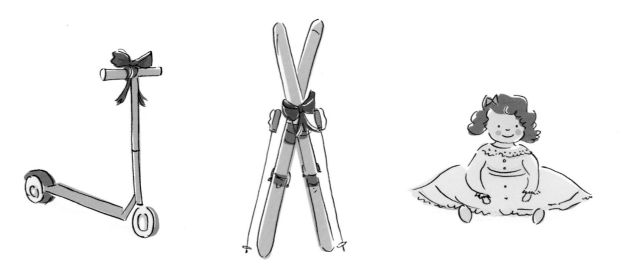

There were even more gifts than the previous year,
which left Santa no time to feed his reindeer.

To make matters worse, the fog was low and thick.
It slowed the sleigh down; Santa had to be quick.

They flew through the sky, circling 'round and around,
but the houses below just could not be found.

Hungry and harried, the deer wanted to split.
But Santa charged on—there was no way he'd quit!

Below, excited children played all together,
except little William, who studied the weather.

Sensing trouble, William formed a smart plan:
"Let's make Reindeer Dust!" And so it began...

The kids would scatter oats, brown sugar and bran
to attract reindeer and one jolly old man.

Magical bags were filled with the sparkling dust,
and the children all hoped, "Will it work? Oh, it must!"

With wishes and dreams, and the clock chiming nine,
the children filed outside and stood in a line.

"Now sprinkle the dust from your bags," William said,
"Just outside of your door and then—quick!—get to bed."

"Before falling asleep on this Christmas Eve, you must say three times, 'I will always BELIEVE!'"

Into their homes the children skipped with a hum,
with great anticipation of Christmas to come.

And just as young William extinguished his light,
a path of dust came alive, and it sparkled bright.

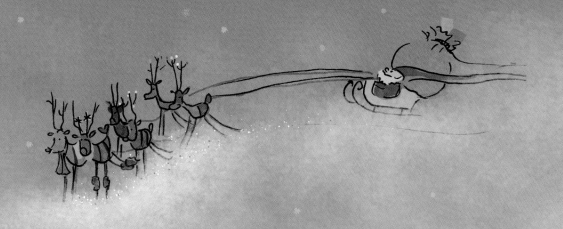

Circling above, the reindeer were relieved to find
the shimmering dust as it glistened and shined.

It danced and it pranced and

lit up the ground.

It skipped and it flipped,

making sure it was found.

Now Santa could reach all the houses with ease,
with presents for all, he was eager to please.

When the children awoke and raced to the tree,
they could hardly contain their genuine glee.

The stockings overflowed with scrumptious treats,
and the sight of their toys made their little hearts beat.

Meanwhile, William peeked outside, delighted to find sparkling hoof prints that had been left behind.

Reindeer Dust Poem

To be read on Christmas Eve as the children spread their reindeer dust.

It's finally time — It's Christmas Eve!
The presents are packed; Santa's ready to leave.

His reindeer are harnessed and ready to go,
with jolly Saint Nick and his sleigh in tow.

Past twinkling stars, through the sky they will roam,
until sparkling dust lights the way to our home.

So, those who believe, form a single line,
and spin around once and then count to nine.

Sprinkle your Reindeer Dust, then off to bed,
for Santa will soon be arriving by sled.

But, before falling asleep on this Christmas Eve,
you must say three times, "I will always BELIEVE!"

Reindeer Dust Recipe

(Makes 15-20 servings)

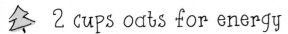 2 cups oats for energy

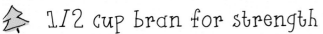 1/2 cup bran for strength

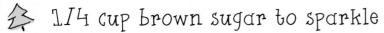 1/4 cup brown sugar to sparkle

 20 small cellophane bags

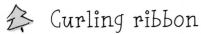 Curling ribbon

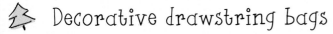 Decorative drawstring bags

Mix together all ingredients.

Scoop 2 tablespoons of mixture into a small cellophane bag.

Tie with a bow.

Insert the cellophane bag into a decorative bag.

Sprinkle the Reindeer Dust on Christmas Eve.

You are now done and ready to share the reindeer fun!